QED Fun with Phonics

Azlo's ABC

Learn the alphabet with Azlo

First published in the UK in 2006 by QED Publishing
A Quarto Group company
226 City Road
London ECIV 2TT
www.qed-publishing.co.uk

A Catalogue record for this book is available from the British Library.

ISBN 1 84538 397 4

Written by Wendy Body
Designed by Alix Wood
Editor Gina Nuttall
Illustrations Caroline Martin

Publisher Steve Evans
Editorial Director Jean Coppendale
Art Director Zeta Davies

Printed and bound in China

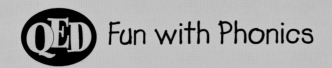

Azlo's ABC

Learn the alphabet with Azlo

Wendy Body

C is for the **caterpillar**
crawling up my wall.

D is for the **dog**
that ran off with my ball.

E is for the "🐝" "elephant" that stepped upon my toe.

8

F is for the **funny face**
that I drew in the snow.

G is for the **goat** that eats everything in sight.

H is for the **hat** that's jammed on really tight.

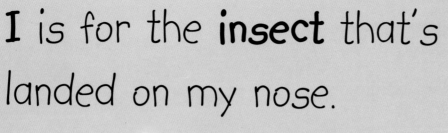 I is for the **insect** that's
landed on my nose.

J is for the
jug of **juice**
that I spilled
on my clothes.

K is for my **kitten** that's sitting on my knee.

L is for the **lion** that's chasing after me.

13

M is for
the **monkey**
with little dancing feet.

N is for the
nuts that the
squirrel likes
to eat.

14

O is for the **octopus**
that invited me for tea.

15

P is for the **pirate** who took me out to sea.

Q is for the **queen** who is making apple pie.

R is for the rainbow stretched across the sky.

S is for the **sun**
that shines when
I go out to play.

T is for the **tiger** that made me run away.

U is for the **umbrella**
that I need in the rain.

V is for the **vase**
I broke playing
with my plane.

Y is for the **yoghurt** I'm eating in this tree.

Z is for the **zebras** that like to play with me.

Parents' and teachers' notes

• Before reading the book, read the title and look at the front cover illustration with your child. Talk about the characters and what they are doing. Which character does your child think is Azlo? (The monster.) Can your child think of anybody he or she knows with a name that begins with the same letter as Azlo?

• As you read the book to your child, run your finger along underneath the text. This will help your child to follow the reading and focus on how the words both look and sound.

• On the first or second rereading, leave out some of the words being used to illustrate the letter sounds and let your child say them. Point to the illustration to help your child supply the word.

• Draw your child's attention to the beginning of words – e.g. "This word begins with an **n** (letter name) and it makes a **nnnnnn** sound." or "This word begins with **s** (letter name) and an **h**. When we put them together they make a **shhh** sound."

• When you are talking about letter sounds, try not to add too much of an **uh** or **er** sound. Say **mmm** instead of **muh** or **mer**, **ssss** instead of **suh** or **ser**. Saying letter sounds as carefully as possible helps children when they are trying to build up or spell words: **fer-o-rer** doesn't sound much like **for**!

• Talk about and discuss the characters on each page – what they look like, what they are doing and why, and what they might be thinking.

• Encourage your child to express opinions and preferences – e.g. "Which picture do you like most?" "Which part of the book did you like best? Why?"

• Choose any page and use the illustration to play "I Spy", using letter sounds rather than names.

• Help your child to make up his or her own alphabet book called "[Your child's name] ABC". Think of a word for each letter of the alphabet. Say the name and sound of each letter as you write it down with the word. Your child might like to draw a picture for each one.

• Say the sound of a letter and ask your child to go on a word hunt to find words in the book that begin with that sound. For the letter **b**, for example, your child might find "bang" and "bed" on page 5, "ball" on page 7 and "broke" on page 20.

• Talk about words: their meaning, how they sound, how they look and how they are spelled. However, if your child gets restless or bored, stop. Enjoyment of the book or activity is essential if we want children to grow up valuing books and reading!